For Matthew, who loves trolleys
—B.C.S.

To Penny
—C.S.

Text copyright © 2016 by Brianna Caplan Sayres
Jacket art and interior illustrations copyright © 2016 by Christian Slade

Visit us on the Web! randomhousekids.com

Educators and librarians, for a variety of teaching tools, visit us at RHTeachersLibrarians.com

Library of Congress Cataloging-in-Publication Data
Sayres, Brianna Caplan.
Where do steam trains sleep at night? / by Brianna Caplan Sayres ; illustrated by Christian Slade. — First edition.
pages cm
Summary: "Imagines the bedtime rituals of different types of trains." —Provided by publisher.
ISBN 978-0-553-52098-9 (trade) — ISBN 978-0-375-97471-7 (lib. bdg.) — ISBN 978-0-553-52099-6 (ebook)
[1. Stories in rhyme. 2. Railroad trains—Fiction. 3. Bedtime—Fiction.] I. Slade, Christian, illustrator. II. Title.
PZ8.3.S274Who 2016
[E]—dc23
2015014342

MANUFACTURED IN CHINA
10 9 8 7 6 5 4 3 2 1
First Edition

Where Do Steam Trains Sleep at Night?

by Brianna Caplan Sayres · illustrated by Christian Slade

Random House New York

Where do steam trains sleep at night
after puffing down the tracks?
Do their moms steam up hot cocoa
for their just-before-bed snacks?

Where do snowplow trains sleep
after all the tracks are clear?
Do their moms say, "Plow your toys, kids—
bedtime's almost here"?

Where do passenger trains sleep
once they've dropped off girls and boys?
Do they fill their seats with teddy bears
and cuddly bedtime toys?

Where do fire trains sleep
when they're heroes of the hour?
Do dads hose them down with water
for a special bedtime shower?

Where do high-speed trains sleep
after a day of crazy speeding?
Do train moms try to calm them down
with sleepy bedtime reading?

Where do breakdown trains sleep
once they've put engines back on rails?
Do their dads rock them off to sleep
with thrilling rescue tales?

Where do trolleys sleep at night
after shuttling through the streets?
Do mama trolleys ring their train bells
for a lullaby, soft and sweet?

Where do subway trains sleep
once they've reached their final stop?
Does the street become their blanket—
a quilt of city lights on top?

Do trains gather in a roundhouse
or a freight yard or a shed?
They don't sleep atop a mattress—
the tracks become their bed!

But they have a special blankie
and an oh-so-bright night-light.
They sleep beneath the crescent moon
and a sky of stars so bright.

Where do your trains sleep at night
when you've drifted off to Dream Land?
Well, maybe all your choo-choos
are fast asleep in Steam Land!